Peter Is Just a Baby

written and illustrated by

Marisabina Russo

Eerdmans Books for Young Readers
Grand Rapids, Michigan • Cambridge, U.K.

Glossary

un (*unh*): one

deux (*deu*): two

trois (*twa*): three

quatre (*kat*): four

cinq (*sank*): five

six (*sees*): six

à la mode: with ice cream

bébé (*bay-bay*): baby

bon anniversaire (*bonh annee-vur-sair*): happy birthday

bon appétit (*bonh ah-peh-tee*): enjoy your meal

bonbons (*bonh-bonh*): candies

c'est la vie (*say la vee*): that's life

merci beaucoup (*mair-see boh-koo*): thank you

mon frère (*monh frair*): my brother

petit chou (*peh-tee shoo*): little cabbage; little darling

petit fours (*peh-tee for*): little cakes

Pierre (*P'yair*): Peter

pirouette (*peer-oo-ett*): ballet turn in which the dancer spins on one foot

quel dommage (*kel doe-mazh*): what a shame

For Jackson

Published in 2012 by Eerdmans Books for Young Readers,
an imprint of Wm. B. Eerdmans Publishing Co.
2140 Oak Industrial Dr. NE
Grand Rapids, Michigan 49505
P.O. Box 163, Cambridge CB3 9PU U.K.

www.eerdmans.com/youngreaders

Manufactured at Tien Wah Press in Singapore in July 2011, first printing

12 13 14 15 16 17 18 19   9 8 7 6 5 4 3 2 1

Library of Congress Cataloging-in-Publication Data

Russo, Marisabina.
Peter is just a baby / written and illustrated by Marisabina Russo.
p. cm.
Summary: A big sister relates some of her accomplishments, which her baby brother is far from able to do.
ISBN 978-0-8028-5384-4 (alk. paper)
[1. Brothers and sisters — Fiction. 2. Babies — Fiction.] I. Title.
PZ7.R9192Pe 2012
[E] — dc23
2011022480

The illustrations were rendered in gouache on watercolor paper.
The display type was set in Sweet Pea.
The text type was set in Century Gothic.

Peter is my brother, and he's just a baby.

He can only say baby words like "baba" when he
wants his bottle and "dada" when he wants Daddy.

Not me.

I can say grown-up words like "manicure" when I want Mama to put pink polish on my nails,

and "skyscraper" when I build a tall tower out of blocks.

I can even count to three in French — *un, deux, trois* — and ask for apple pie *à la mode*.

That's because my grandma has been teaching me French. She tries to teach Peter too, but he just says "baba" again. Then Grandma laughs and calls him her *petit chou*. *Petit chou* means "little cabbage" in French.

Peter is just a baby, and he's a very sloppy eater.

He mashes peas with his spoon.

He gets tomato sauce on his nose.

Sometimes he even gets tomato sauce on his toes.

Not me.

I can balance peas on my tongue.

I can twirl spaghetti around and around my fork without getting a drop of sauce on my nose.

And right before I start to eat, I always say "*Bon appétit!*"

Peter is just a baby, and he can't even walk yet.
He crawls like a little turtle.

Not me.

I can run.

I can leap.

I can skip.

Sometimes I even do *pirouettes* around the living room like a real ballerina.

Ballerinas use lots of French words.

That's one of the reasons I'm going to be a ballerina when I grow up.

Peter is just a baby, and he puts everything in his mouth.

His truck.

His rubber duck.

And even his foot.

Not me.

The only thing I put in my mouth is food.

And my toothbrush.

Actually, sometimes I put the end of a pencil in my mouth, if I'm thinking really hard. And then when I get a good idea, I say "Aha!"

"Aha" isn't a French word, but I think French people probably say it too when they get good ideas. Grandma does.

Peter is just a baby, and he cries all the time.

When he wants to get out of his car seat.

Or his snowsuit.

Or his dirty diaper.

Not me. I only cry about really important things.

Like scraping my knee.

Or saying good-bye to
my cousin at the airport.

Or missing my best friend's birthday party because I've got the chicken pox.

Then I cry and cry and say "*Quel dommage!*" which means "too bad" in French. It's much more dramatic than "too bad" and always gets attention.

Peter is just a baby, and he's never even had a birthday party. He has never worn a party hat or blown out a candle or unwrapped a present.

Not me. I've had one, two, three, four, five, six birthday parties.

one ~ un

two ~ deux

three ~ trois

four ~ quatre

five ~ cinq

six ~ six

I've played musical chairs and pin the tail on the donkey.

I've made wishes and blown out all the candles on my cake with one big puff.

Well, two birthdays ago I didn't blow out all the candles with one big puff.
That was the year I wished for a baby sister. Then I got Peter. *Quel dommage!*

Peter is just a baby, but today he's going to have his first birthday party. Since I'm his big sister, I guess I'll have to help him with everything, like . . .

Putting on his party hat.

Opening his presents.

Making his wishes.

Blowing out his candles.

Happy Birthday, Peter!

Grandma and I both say,
"Bon Anniversaire, Pierre!"

Maybe now that Peter is one year old, he won't act like such a baby anymore.

He'll talk and say words like "bicycle" and "macaroni."

He'll walk and run and do *pirouettes* across the living room floor.

He won't put trucks or ducks or feet in his mouth.

He won't cry unless it's about something very important.

He'll even learn how to speak French, just like me!
Then I'll invite him to my tea parties and
we can eat *petit fours* and *bonbons*.

Bon appétit!

Or maybe I'll have to wait until next year, when he turns *deux*, because for now *Pierre, mon frère*, is still just a *bébé*.

Oh, well. As Grandma says, "*C'est la vie*."